Janet Reachfar and Chickabird

by Jane Duncan

Pictures by Mairi Hedderwick

This edition published in 2002 by
Birlinn Ltd, Edinburgh
Copyright © the Estate of
Jane Duncan 1978
Illustrations copyright ©
Mairi Hedderwick 1978
First published in 1978 by
MacMillan London Limited

ISBN 1 84158 208 5

Birlinn

IT WAS a beautiful bright spring morning on the farm called Reachfar in the Highlands of Scotland, but Janet, who lived there, was in the most terrible temper. Just after breakfast she had run up the farmyard to the moor gate, but before she could climb over it she heard a voice calling, "Janet, come back here this minute!" It was the voice of her grandmother being the stern person that Janet and her friends George and Tom called "Herself". Janet came slowly back down the yard.

"You are not going to run around the moor like a wild hare today," Herself said. "You are a person and not a hare, and people have work to do. Your mother and I are busy in the house, and George and Tom must look to the fencing. Go and lead the horses out of the stable and put them in the west field."

Janet liked her grandmother and all her family and all the animals of Reachfar, but now she felt that she did not like any of them. She wanted to be out on the moor that morning and not helping around the farmyard, but she had to do what Herself said.

She led Betsy from the stable, then Dulcie, then went back for Dick. He was very big and very good-natured, but on this morning he seemed to be feeling a little wild, too. As Janet led him out he danced about on his big hooves, tossing his huge head, and tried to turn the wrong way at the stable door.

"Stop your nonsense, you silly big thing!" Janet said crossly, and slapped him on the nose.

People did not as a rule call Dick silly and slap him, and he was so startled that he did something he had never done before. He went jumping backwards and trod on a half-grown chicken and broke its leg.

Janet felt her bad temper running out through the tips of her toes as George picked up the chicken. "We'll have to kill this bird," he said.

"That is one of the early flock," Tom told him. "Herself will be in a proper rage with us about this." He turned to Janet. "What were you thinking of, slapping Dick like that?"

Janet began to cry. "Don't kill it!" she said. "Please don't kill it!"

"Stop crying," George told her. "All three of us will be crying if Herself comes out and catches us idling about. Go and put Dick in the field and come back to the barn."

When she got back, George was sitting on a heap of
sacks holding the chicken while he and Tom looked at it
sadly. "We'll have to kill it, Janet," Tom said. "The other
grown-up hens will kill it anyway. Birds and animals do not
like sick members of the flock."

Janet felt terrible. She felt that *she* had killed the
chicken. It had been hurt because of her temper. She began
to cry again.

"Stop crying, for pity's sake!" George told her. "Run
along to the house and see what Herself is doing."

Janet stopped crying at once, for she knew that George, now, was not going to kill the chicken. He was going to try to make its leg better so that Herself would never know what had happened.

Janet ran to the house and back to the barn. "She is busy baking," she said.

"Right," said George. "Tom, get me a little
piece of wood to make a splint, and Janet, you
tear up your handkerchief. If Herself notices that it
is gone, you will have to tell a fib and say you have lost it,
and you'll get a scolding for that, but you deserve a scolding
today, anyhow."

Tom and Janet did as he told them, and very soon George had put a little wooden splint on the chicken's leg. Then he handed the bird to Janet.

"You will have to take care of her," he said. "The other hens won't like this splint, and Herself won't like it either. It isn't natural for a chicken to have a wooden leg. You had better take a coop up to the moor and hide her there, and let's hope Herself doesn't notice that one of the flock is missing. But remember, Janet, the leg may not get better. I have never put a splint on a chicken before."

"It *will* get better," Janet said. "It will! It will!"

So Janet hid the chicken on the moor, and for a whole
month she took great care of her. She named her Chickabird,
and carried food secretly to her, wishing and hoping hard all
the time that the leg would get better.

Then, one Sunday, George examined the leg and said, "I think it has mended. We can take the splint off."

Chickabird had grown into quite a big fat brown hen, with a tuft of feathers on top of her head that was a little like Herself's best hat. At first the leg was too weak to hold her up, but soon it grew perfectly strong.

However, she had grown accustomed to her coop up on the moor, and would not come down to the farmyard to be with the other hens or sleep in the hen-house at night. She stayed on the moor by herself, pecking around and growing bigger and fatter and shinier every day.

"When the snow comes she will be glad to come down to the hen-house," Tom said.

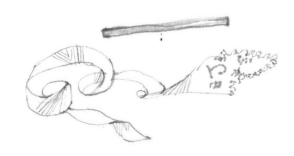

Janet thought so too, for when the winter snow lay deep, many hungry wild creatures came down from the moor – creatures that were never seen near Reachfar house in the summertime.

But when the snow came, Chickabird did not come down. She clucked around her coop and watched the roe deer eat the hay that George, Tom and Janet put out for

them. She cocked her head at the big curlew who came poking about for worms in the mud and slush around the moor pond. She behaved as if she were a special hen, and all the wild creatures were her guests. Janet gave her much more corn than the other hens so that she would have some to spare for any guests who wanted it, like the ugly big black crow that perched on top of her coop.

One morning around Christmas-time, when the snow
was very deep, Janet went up to the moor with some corn
and found that Chickabird had a very special guest. Pecking
around in the snow beside her was a beautiful cock
pheasant with his long tail feathers shining against the snow,
the greenish feathers on his neck gleaming. When his fierce
wild eye saw Janet, he flew away with a loud whirr of his
wings, but after that he was there every morning and
afternoon, sharing Chickabird's corn. Janet hoped he would
grow tame and stay at Reachfar, but George and Tom said
that this would not happen.

"He is wild by nature," George said, "and when spring
comes he will go back to the wild part of the moor."

They were right. One morning, after the snow was gone, Janet went up to the moor with her basket of corn, and the pheasant was gone. But worse, Chickabird was gone too. Janet called and called her, but she did not appear.

"A weasel must have got her," Tom said.

"Or that fox your father saw in the glen last week," said George to Janet. "It was stupid of us to let her stay up here by herself. Tame creatures can't defend themselves in the wild."

"We couldn't help it!" Janet cried. "She wouldn't *stay* in the yard."

By Easter-time Janet had almost forgotten about Chickabird, though the coop still sat among the gorse bushes, and on Easter Sunday Janet decided that she and Fly, her dog, would walk over the moor to see how many wild primroses were in bloom. As they passed the coop, there came from inside it a comfortable clucking noise, then a high cheep-cheeping noise, and a tiny yellowish-brown chicken ran out and back again.

Janet peered in and saw a wonderful sight. There was Chickabird. She stood up, fluffed out her feathers so that she looked very fat, and she looked proud as well as she stepped aside to show Janet her flock of baby chicks. Janet counted twelve of them altogether, but they were not quite like the other yellow chicks down in the farmyard. They were different in the way that the pheasant was different from the farmyard hens and the wild flowers of the moor were different from the flowers in the garden. And then, out of the heather, the cock pheasant rose, flew fast over the coop, his long tail streaming, and away up towards the far part of the moor, calling in his wild harsh voice as he went.

All Janet's family came to see Chickabird and her family.
Herself looked very hard at the coop in the gorse, and then
she looked at George and Tom. "It is a strange thing for a
Reachfar hen to wish to live on this wild moor," she said.
But then she turned into Janet's wise old Granny as she said
to Janet, "It was clever of Chickabird to bring her children
back. She needs you to help her bring them up. They are
only half-wild, and they need us Reachfar people to help
them grow."

After that, Janet was carrying food to the coop several
times a day, for, like their mother, Chickabird's chicks did
not want to come down to the farmyard.
They preferred to stay up on the moor.

"I like them better than Aunt Kate's farmyard chickens,"
Janet told her mother one bedtime. "Do you like them?"

"Yes. I like wild things. Perhaps that is why I like a little
girl who sometimes runs wild on the moor, even though she
comes back for meals in the Reachfar
kitchen," her mother teased.

Janet made a poem about
Chickabird, and this is it:

Chickabird is my pet hen
And once she went away,
But back to Reachfar she did bring
Wild chicks on Easter Day.

"I like them better than Aunt Kate's farmyard chickens," Janet told her mother one bedtime. "Do you like them?"

"Yes. I like wild things. Perhaps that is why I like a little girl who sometimes runs wild on the moor, even though she comes back for meals in the Reachfar kitchen," her mother teased.

Janet made a poem about Chickabird, and this is it:

Chickabird is my pet hen
And once she went away,
But back to Reachfar she did bring
Wild chicks on Easter Day.